To Lilu and Bodhi, for the boundless
love you give to our small army of pets.
—E.L.

For Mom and Dad.
—A.H.

The Perfect Pet for You!
Text copyright © 2021 by Estelle Laure
Illustrations copyright © 2021 by Amy Hevron
All rights reserved. Manufactured in Italy.

ISBN 978-0-06-302599-8

The artist used acrylic paint on wood and pencil to create
the digital illustrations for this book.
Typography by Rachel Zegar
21 22 23 24 25   RTLO   10 9 8 7 6 5 4 3 2 1
❖
First Edition

The Perfect Pet
for
YOU!

story by
Estelle Laure

pictures by
Amy Hevron

HARPER
An Imprint of HarperCollinsPublishers

Hey there!

Are you looking for a pet?

Well, let me help you.

First, don't rush
and don't panic.

That's a very
usual mistake.

Do you like
big animals?

Or small?

Do you need fun tricks?

Or no tricks at all?

Or do you mostly need someone to hold on to when there's a **loud** noise or when you don't feel so good?

Do you want a pet who will say hello to you in the **morning?**

TURTLES

Or who will stay up with you at **night**?

Someone to **snuggle?**

Or **talk** to at a tea party?

Or even one to **ride!**

Maybe one to **slither** around with...

or one who can crawl up the wall with you.

Maybe you need a pet who lives outside
because you wish you lived outside, too.

Or maybe you need a pet who will come for a visit now and again.

There are so many pets to decide between.

And if you get just
the right one, then
you will always have
a best friend.

You will always
have something
to do.

Someone to take
care of, too.

You will not be lonely, and if you are scared, you will know that it's okay because your pet will tell you.

I know it seems like you have to know right away or else maybe your best pet will get chosen by another person.

But it won't, because that is not the way it works.

Your very best pet is only the best for you
and not for anyone else at all.
And it will know. And you will know.

So don't hurry.
Little by little or sometimes quick,
you will get a magic feeling.

THIS
TURTLE!

She is
exactly
perfectly
right
for
YOU!

A turtle goes slow when the world goes fast and you do, too.

She is quiet when the world is loud.

She will let you be alone but not alone alone.
And she will be just next to you when you go deep inside.

She will remind you about fun.
And there will be a little bit more joy.

Because you will be wandering

and wondering

and watching . . .

together.